THE HALLO-WIENER

DAV PILKEY

SCHOLASTIC INC. • NEW YORK TORONTO LONDON AUCKLAND SYDNEY

ISBN 0-590-41729-0

12 11 10 9 8 7 6 5 4 3   10   7 8 9/9 0 1/0

Printed in the United States of America   08

Original Blue Sky Press edition designed by Dav Pilkey and Kathleen Westray

FOR TOM NADRATOWSKI

There once was a dog named Oscar who was half-a-dog tall and one-and-a-half dogs long.

Because of his unusual shape and size,
all the other dogs made fun of him.
"Wiener Dog! Wiener Dog!" they called him.

And Oscar did not like it one bit.

Oscar's mother was no help either. Every morning when the dogs walked off to obedience school, Oscar's mother stood in the front yard waving and calling out, "Farewell, my little Vienna sausage!"

And the other dogs laughed and laughed.

Most of the time, Oscar was upset by all this, but not today. Today was Halloween, and Oscar was thinking about other things. All day long at obedience school, Oscar daydreamed about Halloween night, trick-or-treats, and scary costumes.

When Oscar got home, he dashed upstairs to start working on his scary Halloween costume. But when he got to his room, a surprise was waiting for him.

"Happy Halloween, my little sausage link," said Oscar's mother. "I've made you a costume to wear for trick-or-treats!"

When Oscar saw the costume, he nearly fainted.

It was a giant hot-dog bun, complete with mustard. And guess who was supposed to fit in the middle?

Oscar did not want to hurt his mother's feelings,
so he decided to wear the silly costume.

That night, all the dogs on the block gathered to show off their costumes. Everyone was looking quite scary.

Then Oscar showed up, looking quite frank.

When the dogs saw Oscar in his silly costume, they howled with laughter.

"Look at Oscar," they cried. "He really *is* a Wiener Dog!" Poor Oscar was *so* embarrassed.

"Wiener Dog! Wiener Dog!" laughed the other dogs
as they ran off to go trick-or-treating. Oscar tried
to keep up with the dogs, but his silly costume

All night long the other dogs hounded every treat they could get their paws on.

So by the time Oscar got to each house,
there were no treats left.

Soon trick-or-treating was over, and the
dogs walked home past a spooky graveyard.
Suddenly, a horrible hissing sound filled
the air: "Hsssssssssssssssssssss!"
The dogs stopped dead in their tracks.

Then, out of the graveyard rose a ghastly monster.
The dogs screamed for their lives! They dropped
their treats and jumped into a nearby pond!

The monster moved closer.
"Please don't eat us," cried the dogs.

The monster yowled and hissed.
"Boo-hoo-hoo!" sobbed the dogs.

The monster jumped up and down.
"SOMEBODY SAVE US!" shrieked the dogs.

Just then, *somebody* showed up. It was Oscar.
Because Oscar was so short, he saw something
that the other dogs had not seen. "That's no
monster!" cried Oscar. And with a loud bark,
Oscar waddled to the rescue!

Oscar chomped and tugged with all his might.

R-R-R-R-R-R-R-R-RIP!
And there, standing in the moonlight,
were a couple of ornery *cats*.

"Help!" cried the cats. "We're being attacked by a giant frankfurter!" And they ran off screaming through the graveyard.

The dogs in the pond had seen the whole thing,
and now it was *their* turn to be embarrassed.
"We've been chased into a pond by a couple of
cats!" they moaned.

But Oscar was a true friend. He leaped into
the water and swam out to the dogs.

Oscar's silly costume made a wonderful life raft, and the dogs climbed up.
"All aboard!" Oscar called, and he dog-paddled back to shore.

When they got back to dry land, all the dogs shared their Halloween treats with Oscar.

Because Oscar had been so brave,
the dogs changed his nickname from
"Wiener Dog" to "*Hero* Sandwich."

And from that night on, nobody ever
made fun of Oscar again.